Trash Bash

YOUNG YEARLING BOOKS YOU WILL ENJOY:

The Pee Wee Scout books by Judy Delton

COOKIES AND CRUTCHES
CAMP GHOST-AWAY
LUCKY DOG DAYS
BLUE SKIES, FRENCH FRIES
GRUMPY PUMPKINS
PEANUT-BUTTER PILGRIMS
A PEE WEE CHRISTMAS
THAT MUSHY STUFF
SPRING SPROUTS
THE POOPED TROOP
THE PEE WEE JUBILEE
BAD, BAD BUNNIES
ROSY NOSES, FREEZING TOES
SONNY'S SECRET

Trash
Bash

JUDY DELTON

Illustrated by Alan Tiegreen

A YOUNG YEARLING BOOK

Published by
Dell Publishing
a division of
Bantam Doubleday Dell Publishing Group, Inc.
666 Fifth Avenue
New York, New York 10103

ISBN: 0-440-40592-0

Printed in the United States of America

March 1992

10 9 8 7 6 5 4 3 2 1

CWO

For my favorite grandson,
Daniel Jaschke Levy

Contents

CHAPTER 1

The New Badge

Roger White crawled under the table. He had a long string of firecrackers in his hand. *Pop pop pop* they would go if they were lit. When he got to Rachel Meyers's chair, he dropped the firecrackers under her.

"KaBOOM!" he shouted.

Rachel jumped up. All of the other Pee Wee Scouts jumped up too. They were at Mrs. Peters's house for their meeting. Mrs. Peters was their leader. They met every Tuesday in her basement. The Scouts were seven years old. They were in second grade.

"Roger White, you make me sick!" shouted Rachel.

Her face was white.

Molly Duff put her arm around Rachel. It was no fun to be blown up by Roger. Roger was a bully.

"You're mean," said Tracy Barnes.

"Firecrackers are illegal in our state," said Mary Beth Kelly.

"You are a lawbreaker, Roger. You could be fined a million dollars."

"You could go to jail," said Kevin Moe. "You could be locked up for life."

"They weren't even lit," said Roger. "How come you're scared of itty-bitty firecrackers that aren't even lit?"

Mrs. Peters clapped her hands. She frowned at Roger.

"We don't want any firecrackers in here whether they are lit or unlit," she said. "Pick them up and take them out of here, Roger. Firecrackers can be dangerous."

Everyone sat down again.

"I know that spring is here," Mrs. Peters went on. "But there are lots of ways of celebrating its arrival without firecrackers."

Rachel's hand waved.

"We're having a family picnic this weekend," she said. "I'm making the potato salad all by myself."

Roger made gagging noises. Some of the other Scouts did too.

Mrs. Peters had to clap her hands again.

"We're going to church," said Patty Baker. She and Kenny Baker were twins.

"Why?" said Tim Noon.

"We just are," said Patty.

The Pee Wees all started to talk about where they were going for the weekend.

"We are going to Horseshoe Lake," said Lisa Ronning. "We have a cabin there. There are no firecrackers at the lake."

When the Scouts were finished talking

4

about the weekend, they told all the good deeds they had done during the week. Then they said their pledge. Molly loved their pledge. She loved doing good deeds. She loved coming to Pee Wee Scouts and earning badges. She loved Mrs. Peters's chocolate cupcakes. Being a Pee Wee Scout was the most fun thing about second grade.

"Today," said Mrs. Peters, "we are going to talk about a brand-new badge we are all going to earn."

The Scouts sat up straight. Everyone was listening. Even Roger. They all wanted another badge. They all wanted to know what they had to do to get one. No one could have too many.

"Don't you love collecting badges?" whispered Mary Beth to Molly. She was Molly's best friend.

Molly nodded.

"Spring is a good time to talk about this

badge," said Mrs. Peters. "Roger picked a good day to remind us of it."

Everyone looked at Roger. Mrs. Peters knew how to make everyone feel good. Even if they made trouble.

"When spring comes, we look around our backyards," said Mrs. Peters, "hear birds chirping, and think how important it is to live in a beautiful world. And a clean and healthy world."

"What's the badge?" shouted Sonny Betz. "What's the name of it and how do we get it?"

Mrs. Peters smiled. "The name of our new badge is the Save-the-Earth badge," she said. "Can any of you think of what it means to save the earth?"

"My mom saves coupons," shouted Tim Noon.

The other Scouts snickered.

"His mom saves coupons because they are poor," whispered Tracy to Molly.

"My mom saves coupons, too, and we're not poor," said Molly. "Anyone can save coupons."

"Good, Tim," said Mrs. Peters. "But saving coupons isn't like saving the earth. That kind of saving is collecting. This kind is protecting."

Now a lot of Pee Wee hands were up.

"We have to protect the environment," shouted Kevin. "Or else all the trees and grass and dogs and people will die."

"Cats too," said Mary Beth.

"I'm allergic to cats," said Tracy.

The Pee Wees began to sneeze. Mrs. Peters had to clap her hands again. "Let's stay on the subject of our badges," she said.

Then their leader picked up some chalk and wrote something on the blackboard. "Protect our environment" it said.

"Kevin is right. We have to protect all

living things around us," she said. "Do you have any ideas on how to do that?"

"Pollution," said Kenny Baker. "We can't dump stuff in rivers."

"We can't kill animals," said Molly.

"I killed a fly once," said Sonny.

"A fly isn't an animal, dummy," said Roger. "It's an insect."

"I like flies," said Kenny.

"We have to kill animals," said Lisa. "Like to eat. We have to eat pigs and cows."

"*Mooo, mooo,*" said Tim.

"*Oink, oink, oink,*" said Roger.

Soon all the Pee Wees were mooing and oinking.

"Give me a piece of pig," said Sonny.

"It's not funny," said Molly. "Some people just eat vegetables."

"My uncle is one of those," said Sonny. "He's a veterinarian."

9

"You mean a vegetarian," corrected Mrs. Peters.

Sonny shook his head. "He's an animal doctor, but he eats only beans and peas and junk."

Patty raised her hand. "We shouldn't kill animals to make fur coats," she said. "Like leopards and elephants. Or they'll become distinct."

"Ho, ho," said Roger. "Who wears an elephant coat?"

The Pee Wees began to laugh with Roger.

"Patty is right," said Mrs. Peters. "If we kill rare animals, they will become *extinct.* That means we will never have them on our earth again."

Mrs. Peters wrote *Protect rare animals* on the blackboard. "There are many things we can do to save our earth," she said.

Mrs. Peters told the Scouts about recycling and planting trees. She told them about saving water and conserving energy and not wasting paper.

"A tree has to die so that we can have writing paper," she said.

"We shouldn't have spelling tests," said Roger. "Then we'd save paper!"

"And we shouldn't read books!" said Sonny.

Mrs. Peters frowned at the boys.

"I want you to watch for ways you can help save the earth," she said. "I want you to tell me if you see people polluting or harming nature.

"And I want you each to plant a tree. And collect old newspapers and cans. Keep a list of other things you do every day to save water and energy. Do you know that we have big, big salty oceans, but not much drinking water? We have to take care of our rivers and streams or our drinking water will be gone."

11

The Scouts sat and thought about drinking water. And all the oceans that were salty. What would they do if the rivers dried up? Or if they got clogged up with oil and junk?

"We have to do something!" shouted Molly. "I'm going to start right away."

She wished she could save the earth all by herself. She was glad Mrs. Peters told the class to keep a list. She loved lists. She made lists in notebooks all the time. Lists of her friends' names and addresses. Lists of her favorite jokes. Even grocery lists for her mother.

Now she could make another list. A list of what she did to save the earth. That would be the most important list of all.

CHAPTER 2

Trash Time

Molly wanted to run right out the door and watch for polluters. But the Scout meeting wasn't over. Mrs. Peters was still talking. Talk talk talk. When would she stop?

"Now," said Mrs. Peters at last. "It's time for our treat."

She handed Molly some paper plates. They had blue and yellow flowers on them for spring.

She handed Lisa some napkins. They had green leaves all over them. Even the paper tablecloth had little ladybugs on it.

13

Everyone helped set the table. Then Mrs. Peters brought in a plate of cupcakes with pink, white, and green jelly beans on top of the frosting.

"It's a Save-the-Earth party!" said Mary Beth.

"But a tree got killed to make these plates," said Roger.

The Scouts were shocked. How could Roger accuse Mrs. Peters of destroying the earth?

Their leader smiled. "You are right, Roger. I usually use glass plates. But this is a special occasion."

"If you use real plates, you have to use water to wash them," said Kevin.

Was everyone going after Mrs. Peters today? thought Molly.

"It's better than plastic," said Molly, to make her leader feel better. "Plastic stuff takes about five hundred years to disappear. I saw it on TV."

After the Scouts had their treat, they helped clean up. They washed their hands and faces. Then Mrs. Peters said, "Get into a circle now for our Pee Wee song."

Molly liked the end of the meetings. Before they left they held hands and sang. And Molly loved to sing. She held Mary Beth's hand and squeezed it. Mary Beth was her best friend.

When they finished the song, they ran upstairs and said good-bye to baby Nick. He was just waking up from his nap. He was too little to be a Pee Wee Scout.

"Does Nick wear cloth diapers?" asked Kevin. "Plastic ones pollute. My cousin has a baby and he wears cloth diapers."

"Nick wears cloth diapers," said Mrs. Peters.

Molly felt relieved. She would hate it if the Scouts found Mrs. Peters was polluting again.

*　*　*

Molly ran all the way home to tell her family about the Save-the-Earth badge.

"Mrs. Peters says we have to recycle things," she said.

"Good," said Mr. Duff. "Make something work twice, is what I always say. Use things over and over again."

Molly went up to her room. She got out her notebook. Her father was right. Recycling was using something over and over. What could she use over and over?

She looked into her wastebasket. There was a piece of paper in it. It had writing on only one side. She took it out of the wastebasket. She would make her list on that, instead of on a new piece of notebook paper.

There was a hair ribbon in the wastebasket too. It was wrinkled. She would press it flat between two books and use it again.

"There must be lots of things in other people's wastebaskets," she said out loud. "Things that could be used."

She picked up her pencil and wrote, *Use trash.*

Molly picked up her phone and called Mary Beth. "I have an idea," she said. "Come over and I'll tell you about it."

Mary Beth came right over.

"Everybody in town has wastebaskets," said Molly. "I think we should stop them before the garbage truck takes the stuff away. It's up to us to use all that stuff again."

"There's a lot of garbage in town," said Mary Beth doubtfully. "Can we use it all?"

"We have to!" said Molly. "If they don't recycle, it's up to us!"

Molly was fired up with excitement. This was a big responsibility. She wasn't a Pee Wee Scout for nothing. Maybe adults were not saving the earth, but surely a Pee Wee Scout had to.

"We need help," said Mary Beth. "We can't do this alone. Look at all those houses. They all have lots of trash. And we can't just go in and grab their wastebaskets."

Molly thought about that. "We can collect it when they put it in the alley for the garbageman," she said. "And I suppose Lisa could help us."

On the way to Lisa's house, the girls met Rachel.

"I'm going to recharge old batteries," she said.

"Pooh," said Mary Beth. "We are going to recycle trash. We're going to make something new out of stuff like this egg carton."

Mary Beth kicked an old egg carton that had fallen out of a Dumpster.

"Like what?" asked Rachel.

"Like a jewelry box," said Molly. "This egg carton could be a jewelry box. All we have to do is paint it."

Rachel looked doubtful. But she said, "Can I help?"

Molly wanted to save the earth by herself. But she knew that was selfish. Besides, as Mary Beth had said, it was too much for one person.

"Okay," she said. "But we have to get started right away."

"Let's get paint," said Rachel. "We can make a jewelry box right away."

"I think we have to collect the stuff first," said Mary Beth. "Before the garbageman takes it and dumps it in the river. Once we save all this valuable stuff, then we can make new things out of it."

Mary Beth was very wise, thought Molly. First things first.

"I'll go get my wagon," said Molly.

"I'll get my bike. It's got two baskets on it," said Rachel.

"I'll get my mom's grocery cart," said Mary Beth. "And then we'll meet back here in ten minutes."

The girls forgot about getting Lisa. They raced home to get wheels. They raced back and got to work. They went up one alley and down another.

"This feels like stealing," said Mary Beth softly.

"It's the opposite of stealing," said Molly. "We are doing something good. We are saving the earth."

Rachel placed an old bike tire in Mary Beth's shopping cart.

Mary Beth opened a big plastic bag and took out a dish that was chipped.

Molly found a doll with a missing arm. And a teddy bear with no eyes.

"We could sell some of this stuff," she whispered.

"We don't want to make money," said Rachel. "We want to recycle."

"What can we make out of this old light bulb?" asked Molly.

"A nose for a snowman," said Mary Beth. "We'll paint it red next winter."

The girls opened bag after bag. They filled their wagon and bike baskets and shopping cart to overflowing. They were hot and dirty and tired.

"I think we should stop for today," said Molly. "It's getting dark. Let's meet tomorrow and go down Elm Street."

The girls wheeled the trash back to Molly's house.

"Let's put it behind the garage," said Molly.

Even though she knew her dad would be pleased to know she was saving the earth,

she wasn't sure he'd like to see the drive-
way full of junk.

"Saving the earth is hard work," said
Mary Beth, throwing herself on Molly's
front lawn to rest.

"It's worth it," said Molly. "See you guys
out here tomorrow morning."

CHAPTER 3

Cartons and Curtains

The next morning Molly and Mary Beth and Rachel met on Elm Street. Some of the other Pee Wees were looking for trash too.

"Look at this eggbeater I found," said Lisa. "It really turns. I'm going to recycle it."

"It's all rusty and dirty," said Rachel.

"You can still sell it for scrap metal," said Kevin. "I've got a whole bag of old nails and junk to turn in."

The Pee Wees pulled their wagons down

alleys. They pushed their bikes up hills. They had bags and bags of trash. They put them behind Molly's garage and then went out for more.

By the next Pee Wee meeting, they had lots and lots of trash.

"Have you been working hard to save the earth?" asked Mrs. Peters when she greeted them.

All the Pee Wees talked at once.

"I put a brick in the tank of our toilet, to save water, Mrs. Peters," said Patty.

"That's nothing," said Roger. "I put a brick in lots of toilets. My grandma's and my aunt's and my cousin's."

"I hope you asked them first," said Mrs. Peters.

"I planted my tree already," said Rachel. "A weeping willow."

"Why is it weeping?" asked Tim.

"Probably because it didn't want to be in Rachel's yard!" shouted Roger.

Rachel ignored Roger. Maybe she didn't hear him, thought Molly. But Roger picked on Rachel. He loved to make her mad.

"Good for you, Rachel," said Mrs. Peters.

"I stopped a lady on the street," said Kevin. "She was smoking. I told her she was polluting her body."

The Pee Wees cheered.

"We must be careful not to be rude," said Mrs. Peters. "Try not to step on toes."

"Did you step on her toes, Kevin?" asked Tim.

"That's just an expression, silly," said Rachel.

Roger's hand was waving.

"I stopped using paper towels," he said. "Because of the trees."

"He wipes his hands on his shirt instead, Mrs. Peters! I saw him," shouted Sonny.

Roger gave Sonny a mean look.

"Well, you did. It's the truth," said Sonny.

"I brush my teeth without water," said Kenny proudly.

"Yuck!" said Lisa. "How do you rinse the toothpaste out of your mouth? Is your mouth all white inside?"

All the Pee Wees ran over to Kenny to look in his mouth.

"It isn't," he said.

"You swallowed it! Gross!" cried Rachel.

Molly told about all the trash they had collected for recycling. "We are going to use it twice," she said.

"Good for you," said Mrs. Peters. "There will be a prize for the one who does the most creative thing with trash," she added.

Now Molly's mind was really spinning. Maybe an egg carton jewelry box wasn't creative enough. She had to find something no one else would think of. She had to win that prize!

Mrs. Peters talked some more about recycling. She talked about trees and water and pollution and clean air. She showed them the Save-the-Earth badge. And she showed them a short film about endangered species.

"I'm glad you all had so many things to report," she said.

The Scouts sang their song and said their pledge. They played games and played with baby Nick. Then they had ginger cookies and milk.

"Next week we'll give the prize for the most creative recycling," said Mrs. Peters as they left. "And then we'll have a campaign to collect old newspapers."

"I think we have enough trash," said Mary Beth. "Come and see what we've got," she said to the boys, on the way to Molly's. "We better start recycling it."

When the Scouts got to Molly's house, Molly's mother said, "What are all those bags behind the garage?"

Molly told her.

"It's good to recycle," said Mrs. Duff. "But those bags are killing the grass and they will attract mice."

Mary Beth was right. It was time to put this trash to a new use.

Lisa held up an old hot-water bottle.

"I'll bet it leaks," said Molly.

"It must be good for something," said Tracy.

"I'm going to use these buttons," said Lisa. "They are perfectly good buttons and someone threw them away."

"They're all different colors," said Mary Beth. "You can't wear a blouse with all different kinds of buttons on it."

"I'm not putting them on a blouse," said Lisa mysteriously.

"Tell us!" shouted Tim.

Lisa shook her head. She picked all the buttons out of the trash and put them into her pocket.

"Here's a doorbell!" shouted Kenny. "I'm going to put it on my door."

"We have a doorbell already," Patty reminded him.

"Two is better," said Kenny.

All the Pee Wees found something to recycle.

"Let's go down in my basement and make this stuff," said Molly.

The Scouts took what they had found and followed Molly. Each one wanted to win Mrs. Peters's prize.

Kenny worked on the old doorbell.

Lisa worked with her buttons and some old wire.

Tracy decided to make earrings out of some small springs she found.

"I can paint them with colored nail polish!" she said.

Molly looked and looked through a big trash bag. She was still looking for something special. Something that no one else would think of. Something good enough to win the prize.

Not jewelry.

Not doorbells.

Not egg carton jewelry boxes.

All of a sudden she saw something. It was in the bottom of the bag. It was white. When she pulled it up, she saw that it was a curtain. A long white lace curtain. And underneath it were some more curtains just like it.

"Ooh," said Mary Beth. "Those look brand-new! I wish I'd found them. I'd make a doll dress."

"There are too many for a doll dress," said Molly. "I am going to make a dress for me. A lace dress."

Now the other girls wanted to make dresses. But Molly had found the best material.

"Ho, you can't sew," said Roger. "You need a sewing machine to make a dress."

"Do not," said Molly, even though what Roger said sounded true.

"I'll use pins."

Molly ran upstairs and got her mother's pincushion. She held the curtains up in front of her. She folded them and gathered them and tucked them. She used lots and lots of pins.

The curtains were long. They went to the floor, even with pins in them. The sleeves hung down to Molly's fingertips.

"It looks beautiful!" said Tracy.

"It looks like you are wearing curtains,"

said Roger. "Ha, ha, Molly's a window! Molly's a window!"

"I think it looks too pretty to wear for every day," said Mary Beth. "It should be for a fancy party."

Molly's heart jumped. It would be a wedding dress! It was white and it was lace. Mrs. Peters would be very proud of her! She would say, Look at Molly! She has made her own wedding dress!

A wedding dress was very, very creative. No other Scout would make her own wedding dress. Molly was sure to be the only one. Unless she told them what she was doing. And she wouldn't. It would be her secret. She would finish it after everyone had gone.

She took the dress off and pretended to be interested in what the others were doing. But inside she had her own warm little secret. This wedding dress would make her a winner.

"Look," said Tracy. She hooked her spring earrings behind her ears and they bobbed up and down. The metal showed through even though she'd used three coats of nail polish.

She'll never win, thought Molly. No way.

"They are pretty," she told Tracy. "They bounce like little curls."

Lisa's button secret turned out to be buttons on wire. She strung them in a row and then put it around her arm for a bracelet.

"That's smart," said Molly. But not smart enough to win, she wanted to add.

Kenny's doorbell wouldn't ring. "I have to get a battery," he said.

Rachel was painting her egg carton with an old can of spray paint. It was pretty but not pretty enough. It was no wedding dress, that was for sure.

"We have to go home and eat," said Kenny. "We can finish tomorrow."

As soon as the Scouts left, Molly worked on her dress. "I'll be older and bigger when I get married," she said out loud to herself. "I better make this gown longer and fatter."

Molly let three pins out in the waist. She made the sleeves fatter and the hem longer. Then she made a veil for her head, and a long train that dragged on the floor in back of her. Just like a real bride, she thought.

She ran to her drawer and got some hair ribbons. She tied them on the sleeves. She put one long one around her waist. She got some of her mother's artificial flowers from a vase in the living room. She pinned them to her belt and on the top of her head.

When she looked in the mirror, she was shocked.

"I'm a real bride!" she said out loud.

She wanted to rush right over to Mrs. Peters and show her. But it was too late.

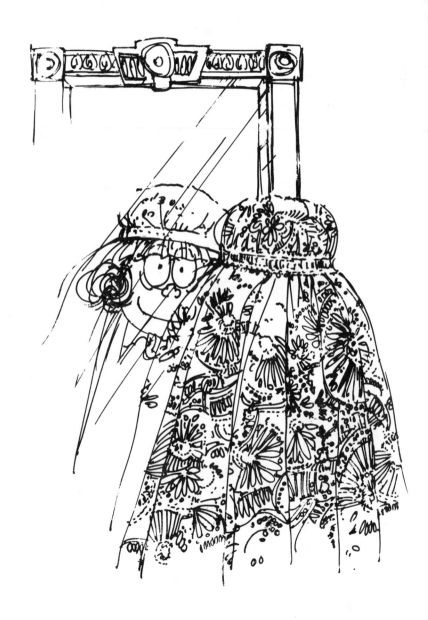

Mrs. Peters might be in bed. Molly had done what her father said, used something twice. She definitely was saving the earth. She thought of all those wasted new wedding dresses, and she, Molly, would put a label in hers that said MADE WITH 100 PERCENT RECYCLED GOODS. She was bursting with pride. What was an old egg carton compared to a wedding gown?

And besides saving the earth, she'd win a prize. She didn't ever remember being so happy or so patriotic.

She took her dress off and folded it carefully. The sooner she got to bed and fell asleep, the sooner the Pee Wee meeting would come.

CHAPTER 4

Molly Is a Window

It seemed to take forever, but finally Tuesday came. Molly took her recycled curtain dress to the meeting in a big box. She would put it on in Mrs. Peters's bathroom.

All of the Pee Wees were carrying things.

Tracy had on her bobbing-spring earrings.

Lisa wore her button bracelet.

Kenny was ringing his doorbell.

And Rachel's jewelry box still looked like an egg carton.

"Now!" said Mrs. Peters. "I can't wait to see what my Scouts have done to recycle!"

Everyone's hand was waving.

The prize was in a bag in front of Mrs. Peters.

"I'll bet it's a book," whispered Patty. "A book about saving the earth."

"It looks more like a game," said Kevin. "One of those new ecology games."

"Let's start with Tim," said Mrs. Peters.

Molly liked the way Mrs. Peters started with shy people. People who didn't wave their hands.

Tim held up money he had gotten from cans and scrap metal he had collected and turned in.

"Good for you." Mrs. Peters smiled at Tim. "If everyone collected metal, the earth wouldn't run short."

"But he didn't actually recycle it himself, Mrs. Peters," said Rachel.

"There are many ways of recycling, Rachel," said Mrs. Peters.

"She likes their way better," whispered Rachel to Molly. "She didn't make that much fuss over my jewelry box when I came in."

It was just like school, thought Molly. Trying to know what the teacher wanted. It was a full-time job for a second-grader.

Mrs. Peters called on Tracy. She showed her jumpy earrings.

Lisa showed her button bracelet.

All the Scouts took their turns. Molly wanted to be last. The best for last. Mrs. Peters looked at old lampshades made into funny hats. She saw belts made into dog collars.

"Let's have a little break before we hear from Mary Beth and Molly," said Mrs. Peters. "We could use a cold drink."

Was Mrs. Peters getting tired? Bored? Had she seen enough old junk for the day? Maybe Nick would wake up and distract her. Maybe the time would be up and

Molly would have to wait until next week! Maybe Mary Beth would take too long with her turn.

It took a long time for the Pee Wees to drink their sodas. Roger took ages collecting the cans and straws. Mrs. Peters took ages putting the soda cans into the machine that squished them flat. Twelve cans. One by one by one.

Mrs. Peters began to talk about acid rain. Had she forgotten about recycling?

"Mrs. Peters," called Mary Beth at last. "Can I show what I recycled?"

"Oh, yes," said their leader. "We still have you and—"

"And Molly," said Mary Beth.

That was loyal of Mary Beth to remember her. Mary Beth was a loyal best friend.

Mary Beth reached under the table for a big, big package she had with her. She took it out and held it up.

It looked like a person! Was it all right to make a person out of trash?

"It's a scarecrow!" blurted out Mary Beth proudly. "It's an old mop for a head, and a stick for a body. I found this old dress in the trash, and the hat and the old necklace. Then I tied these old cans on the skirt so when it flapped in the wind the noise would scare the crows away from a garden."

Mrs. Peters looked impressed. "Mary Beth has used the most old things in her project," she said. "Just look at all the old things on her scarecrow."

"I got the idea from Molly," said Mary Beth. "Instead of just a dress, I thought I'd use lots of old things."

Copycat! thought Molly. And what does she mean, "just a dress"? She had given Molly's idea away. It would not be a surprise anymore. What kind of a best friend was this anyway?

46

"Are there crows in your yard?" asked Rachel.

Mary Beth shook her head. "But there could be," she added.

"Have you got a garden?" demanded Roger.

"Well no, but . . ." said Mary Beth.

"Ho, no garden, no crows! What good's something to scare crows if there are no crows!" he chortled.

"I can give it to a farmer," said Mary Beth. She looked as if she might cry.

Molly wished she wasn't last. Everyone was restless. They wanted to go home.

"All right, Molly. Let's see what you have," said Mrs. Peters.

Molly went into the bathroom and put on her dress and veil.

She pinned it the way she had at home. But it didn't look as good as it did in her bedroom mirror. The sleeves were different lengths and she had forgotten the flowers. The veil didn't stay on and there was a spot on one of the curtains that Molly had not seen before. It looked like catsup.

"Hurry up!" she could hear Roger shouting. "Are you melting down tin cans or what?"

When Molly came out, everyone stared. No one said anything. Maybe they were overcome with her beauty, Molly thought.

"It's those curtains," Roger finally said. "Molly's recycled into a window!"

Everyone in the room began to laugh. Not a little laugh. Not a chuckle. But a big holding-your-breath kind of laugh. Even Mrs. Peters was trying not to laugh.

"It's not a window!" said Molly. "It's a wedding gown! I made a wedding gown from old curtains!"

Mrs. Peters clapped her hands. She tried to frown.

"It's very unusual," she said.

Kenny held his doorbell up to his stomach. "Look, guys, I'm a door!" he said.

"Let's not tease Molly," said Mrs. Peters, holding up her hand. "It is sort of recycling. You are on the right track, Molly," she went on.

"Yeah, but you've got the wrong engine!" shouted Kevin.

"I was thinking of something more—practical," said Mrs. Peters.

Molly sat down. The pins were sticking her. She was afraid she would cry.

"I think the winner is Mary Beth," said Mrs. Peters. "All your things were wonderful, but Mary Beth used the most items. And second prize goes to Tim, who sold the most scrap metal," she said.

Her best friend, Mary Beth, had won the prize. And she, Molly the earthsaver, had not even come in second! Old tin cans had come in ahead of her beautiful wedding dress! Maybe Mrs. Peters did not understand that Molly was going to *wear* this dress. To really get married in it someday. Why else would she have made it so large?

But everyone was gathered around the winners. Making a fuss over a dingy scarecrow. And a bunch of old cans.

Molly wasn't sure she wanted to save the earth anymore. She would just put those curtains back in the garbage.

Not only had she lost the prize. She might even have lost her best friend.

CHAPTER **5**

Save Those Trees!

Mary Beth opened her prize.

It wasn't a game.

It wasn't a book.

"A can crusher!" shouted Mary Beth. "Just what I wanted!"

"Now you can crush your own soda cans," said Mrs. Peters.

"I'll let you use it too," said Mary Beth to Molly. "You can come over to my house and crush your cans."

Molly did not want to share a prize. She didn't want Mary Beth to feel sorry for her.

The second prize went to Tim. He got a little tree.

"It is a little pine sapling," said Mrs. Peters. "You can plant it in your backyard and watch it grow."

Tim touched the tree's green needles.

"It'll be a Christmas tree," said Kevin. "You can decorate it at Christmas and you won't have to cut down a real one."

"And now, before our pledge and our song, I want to tell you about our next Save-the-Earth project. Newspapers!"

The Pee Wees cheered. All except Molly. She wasn't going to get excited about a bunch of old papers.

"This week we'll collect them and tie them in bundles and take them to a paper company for recycling. Your newspapers will have a whole new life as a grocery bag or a notebook or a paper cup!"

"Hip hip hooray!" shouted Kevin.

The Scouts said their pledge and sang their song.

Molly put her dress in the box and started home.

"I really liked your wedding dress," said Patty on the way. "I think you should have won."

"I do too," said Mary Beth, putting her arm around Molly. "I wouldn't have thought of a scarecrow if it wasn't for you."

"What's in the box?" asked Molly's mother when she got home.

Molly showed her family the wedding dress.

"I saved the old curtains," she said. "But I didn't win."

Molly's mother put her arm around her.

"It is very creative," she said.

"But I hope you don't plan on wearing it soon," said Mr. Duff. "I'd hate to lose my daughter to Roger White at this young age."

Molly laughed at her father's words. The picture of her marrying Roger in second grade was funny. Marrying Roger anytime was funny. If she married anyone in that dress, it would be Kevin.

The next day Molly felt better. The wedding dress didn't seem as important. When she tried it on again, it looked pretty funny.

Maybe she would collect a few newspapers to save a tree. But just a few.

She called Mary Beth, but Mary Beth had to go to her aunt's house for a few days.

"It's a family reunion," she said.

But Sonny and Roger said they could use some help. Sonny's new father, Larry Stone, said he would go along with them and let them load newspapers into his fire truck.

"Maybe I'll be better at collecting papers than I was at recycling," said Molly to herself.

"Remember to be polite," said Mrs. Peters as the Pee Wees set out on Tuesday afternoon after their meeting. "Even if the people don't have any newspapers, be sure and thank them."

"My dad is taking us," said Patty. "In his truck."

"My dad is picking up our papers in the fire truck," boasted Sonny.

Molly went to the houses on one side of Elm Street.

Roger went to the houses on the other side.

Sonny said he didn't like to knock on people's doors except on Halloween.

"We don't get a newspaper," said a lady at the first house Molly went to. "Bad news, that's all that is in the newspaper. Bad news."

Molly wanted to tell her about the comics and the movie guide to family entertainment, but she remembered about being polite. So she just nodded. And said thank you. Then she went to the house next door.

"We are collecting newspapers to make bags and notebooks out of," said Molly to the man at the door. He looked as if he had been taking a nap. "We are saving the earth."

The man stretched. "There are some in the basement," he said. He pointed to a door.

Molly ran to get Sonny, and the two of them carried piles and piles of papers out of the house to where Mr. Stone was waiting.

"We cleaned out his basement for him," said Sonny. "I think that's a good deed."

Roger lugged newspapers out of another basement. One lady sent them up to the attic.

The pile of papers grew. It got higher and higher.

"Is your dad going to put the siren on?" asked Roger.

"Not unless the newspapers catch on fire," said Sonny.

Larry and the Scouts loaded the papers into his truck and drove to another street. They carried out piles and piles of papers.

"Rachel is right, this is dirty work," said Molly, looking at her black hands.

"I'm pooped," said Roger, throwing himself on someone's front lawn.

Larry loaded more papers into the fire truck. "Tomorrow morning you'll have to tie them up," he said. "I've got some rope down at the station."

Molly was hot and tired and dirty. Her mother ran a nice warm bath for her when she got home.

"We got a lot of papers," said Molly.

"Maybe you'll win this time," said her mother. "And if you don't, you'll still get your badge."

Molly was too tired to care about winning. She was just glad she was helping to save some nice green trees. Trees that had swings on them for children to play on. And trees that made shade to sit under on a hot day. Maybe one of the trees she'd saved was the big oak in the park that the Scouts climbed in. Or the one in Kevin's backyard with a tree house in it!

In the morning Molly met Roger and Sonny and went to the fire station. Larry showed them how to stack the newspapers in small piles and tie them tightly.

"This will take forever!" cried Roger.

"The paper company won't take loose papers," said Larry. "They'd blow all over the place. And they couldn't weigh them."

Molly sat and stacked and tied. Stacked and tied. Paper by paper. She read things out loud as she worked.

" 'Man goes to jail for robbery,' " she read. " 'Interest rates go up in August.' "

"Boring," said Roger.

"Not for the robber," said Molly.

Some of the other Pee Wees came by as they worked.

They came in and tied up their papers too. Their hands got smudged from the ink.

"Larry should get a badge too," said Lisa. "For all the rope he got us."

"He's got a badge," said Sonny. "A fire badge. That's better than a Scout badge."

The Pee Wees laughed. But Molly knew a Scout badge was just as important as a fire badge.

The Scouts tied and tied, but there still were mountains of papers left. Papers were boring. Roger was right. They all looked alike.

All of a sudden Molly came to a different kind of paper.

It was smaller.

It was cleaner.
It had numbers on it.
And it had names on it.
Names of people, signed in ink.

CHAPTER 6

The Un-newspaper

"**L**ook!" said Molly.

She held up the paper that was not a newspaper.

Roger came and felt the paper.

"It's real paper," he said. "Tie it up. It probably doesn't weigh much, though."

"Just a minute," said Larry. He took the paper from Molly and looked at it.

Then he whistled.

"This isn't just paper," he said. "It's a government bond. It is worth a lot of money. Molly found an important paper."

Everyone looked at Molly with admiration. Her face turned red.

"And Roger wanted to tie it up with the newspapers!" cried Tracy.

Now Roger turned red. "I don't know about government stuff," he said.

"I wonder who this came from," said Larry thoughtfully.

He tapped the paper on the table.

"It must have been in with the newspapers you collected. But which house is it from?"

"Maybe it was on Elm Street," said Molly. "Roger and Sonny and I went up and down Elm Street."

"It came from Elm Street," said Roger, nodding.

"But it might have been in with the papers we collected!" said Lisa. "Our papers are all mixed together."

Larry went to get the phone book.

"This bond is made out to Harold Gale," he said, running his finger down the list of G's.

He shook his head. "There is no Gale," he said.

Everyone sat and thought about what to do.

"It has to be from one of the houses we went to," said Molly. "Maybe we should go back and ask all the people we collected papers from if they lost something valuable."

Roger groaned. "That's a lot of houses. I'm not doing that all over again."

"There might be a reward," said Sonny.

Roger got to his feet. "I'll check Elm Street," he said.

Larry laughed. "We can't count on a reward," he said. "We have to do this because this bond belongs to someone and it is valuable. It may be someone's nest egg."

"It doesn't look like an egg to me," said Tim. "If it is, it's old and rotten."

"We had a rotten egg in our refrigerator once," said Sonny. "Yuck, it smelled awful."

Sonny held his nose. Then all of the Pee Wees started to laugh and hold their noses.

"A nest egg is someone's savings," said Larry. "It may be all the money Harold Gale has in the world."

Molly began to feel sorry for Harold Gale. Maybe at this very moment he did not have any cornflakes or milk in his house. Maybe he could not pay his rent, and would go to jail.

"We have to find him!" said Molly, standing up and ready to look.

"I'll give Mrs. Peters a call," said Larry.

Mrs. Peters came as soon as baby Nick woke up from his nap.

Before long, the Pee Wees were back on

Elm Street. They retraced their steps. They went to every house they remembered going to before.

"Is your name Harold Gale?" said Molly politely, to every man who came to the door.

They all said no.

All the ladies said they never heard of Harold Gale.

"Hey, we should wait till it rains," said Roger when the Scouts met back at the fire station. "When it thunders and storms, there could be a gale!"

"Ha, ha, ha," said Kevin. "Very funny, White."

"Hey, if there is no Harold Gale, does Molly get to keep the money? Can she divide it with all of Troop Twenty-three?" asked Sonny.

"We could buy lots of treats for our meetings," said Tim.

"We could buy trees to plant," said Kevin.

"I think we should get a car," said Roger. "A real fast red race car so we could go to Scout camp in it."

"We can't all fit in one car," said Patty.

"Then let's get two!" said Kenny.

Mrs. Peters and Larry both held up their hands.

"The money belongs to Mr. Gale," said Larry.

"It's up to us to find him and return it to him," added Mrs. Peters.

The Pee Wees sighed. A red car with PEE WEE SCOUTS on the side of it would have been fun.

"There is no Harold Gale," said Lisa. "We went to every house."

All of a sudden Molly remembered something. She hadn't gone to every house. She hadn't gone back to the sleepy man's house. To the first house where she'd got papers. Could his name be Mr. Gale?

He didn't look poor. But he was thin. Maybe he had no food to eat because the Scouts had taken his money.

"Just a minute!" said Molly.

She raced back to Elm Street. She found the sleepy man's house and ran up the steps. She rang the doorbell.

No one answered.

She rang it again.

At last the sleepy man came to the door. He yawned.

"I gave you papers yesterday," he said.

"Are you Mr. Gale?" asked Molly.

The man shook his head.

"No," he said. "I'm Jack Olson."

Molly's face fell. This man was their last hope. If he wasn't Mr. Gale, who was? Molly had found the government bond, it was up to her to return it.

71

"Harold Gale is my uncle," said Jack Olson. "Why do you want him?"

Molly couldn't believe her ears! How had his uncle's money gotten in Mr. Olson's old newspapers?

Molly told him about the government bond.

"It was in the pile of newspapers you gave us," she said.

Jack Olson didn't look sleepy anymore. He was wide-awake now.

"We've been looking for that bond for weeks," he said. "We thought it was gone forever. We thought someone stole it."

Molly ran to get Mrs. Peters and Larry, and the other Pee Wee Scouts.

"My uncle brought some papers over to my house to sign," said Jack Olson, when the group returned to his house. "The bond must have been with them. Somehow it got in with the old newspapers on the table," he explained.

Jack Olson called his uncle on the telephone.

"He wants to give you a reward," said Mr. Olson.

"No reward is necessary," said Mrs. Peters. "It is a Scout's job to help others."

The Scouts groaned. What was wrong with a little reward?

Larry and Mrs. Peters and Jack Olson and the Scouts went back to the fire station. Molly handed over the bond she had found to Jack Olson.

"My uncle will want to thank you himself," he said. "But at least let me treat the Scouts to dairy cones."

"Yeah!" said Tim.

"It's not a red race car," said Roger. "But it's better than nothing!"

Molly knew what kind of cone she would order.

Vanilla with chocolate sprinkles.

CHAPTER **7**

Batman Molly

PEE WEE SCOUT DOES GOOD DEED, read the newspaper the next evening.

"You are famous!" said Mary Beth to Molly on the telephone.

"Good for you, Molly," said Mr. Duff when he read it. "Mr. Gale said if you had not collected papers for your Save-the-Earth badge, he never would have found his money. Besides saving the earth, you did a good deed."

"Mr. Gale is donating money to the camp fund," said Mrs. Peters, who called next. "We are so proud of you, Molly."

Next Tuesday at the Pee Wee meeting, all the Scouts had the news clipping with Molly's picture in it.

"It's like being a movie star," said Tracy.

"My cousin was in the paper once," said Rachel. "She was a flower girl in a wedding."

"This is better," said Mary Beth loyally. "Because it's for a good deed."

"It's a good deed to be a flower girl," said Rachel.

The Pee Wees booed.

"Mrs. Peters, isn't being a flower girl a good deed?" asked Rachel.

"I'm sure your cousin was a very pretty flower girl, but I'm not sure it is a good deed," replied Mrs. Peters.

Roger made a face at Rachel. "See?" he hissed.

Mrs. Peters tapped a pencil on the table.

"Today," she said, "we get our Save-the-Earth badges."

Everyone cheered. "Yeah!" they called.

"Everyone has done something to save our earth in the last few weeks," she went on. "Some have done a little." The Scouts looked around the room. "And some have done a lot." The Scouts looked at Molly and Mary Beth and Tim. "But everyone has done something."

Mrs. Peters called out names and the Pee Wees got their badges. On the badge was a little globe with a tree in it. The Scouts pinned them onto their shirts. The badges were blue and green.

"And now we have a little prize for the one who collected the most papers," said Mrs. Peters.

Mrs. Peters gave a package to Kevin.

"That's not fair, your mom works for a newspaper!" shouted Roger. "She brought those home from work for you."

"Is that fair?" cried Lisa.

"It doesn't matter where the papers came from," said Mrs. Peters. "You all worked very hard, but Kevin did bring in the most."

The prize was another can crusher.

Molly felt a little disappointed for the second time. But it was true, she had not had the most papers. And no one else got her picture in the paper. That was like a prize. And making Mr. Gale happy was a prize. She could always save her money and buy a can crusher.

The Scouts played games and sang songs. They had chocolate cake and ice cream and played with baby Nick. They told the good deeds they had done.

Before they left, Mrs. Peters said, "Now remember, boys and girls, we are not through saving the earth just because we got our badges. Saving the earth is a lifetime job. Keep recycling, keep planting trees, keep conserving water, and watch for polluters."

Molly felt tired. It was a big job. And it wasn't over.

Mary Beth and Molly and Rachel walked home together.

"We've got a lot of badges," said Mary Beth.

"Yes, we have," agreed Molly. What if Mrs. Peters wanted the Scouts to recycle them? Molly hoped not.

"Look!" said Mary Beth. She pointed to a man in his yard. He was spraying his fruit trees with a little machine.

"We have to stop him," she said. "That stuff poisons the insects, and the birds eat the insects and get sick."

"We have our badges," said Rachel. "I'm going home to sew mine on my blouse."

"You heard Mrs. Peters," said Mary Beth, stamping her foot. "We can't stop saving the earth just because we have a badge."

Molly knew she was right. But she felt like Rachel. She wanted to go home and forget the sick birds.

"Come on," said Mary Beth, dragging Molly and Rachel with her into the man's yard.

"Stop!" she called out to the man.

"What is it?" he asked.

"Stop spraying those trees," she called. "That stuff poisons the insects and the birds eat them and they get sick."

The man kept spraying.

"If I don't spray my trees, the fruit will die," said the man.

"He's right," said Rachel. "He could have sick trees. That's just as bad as a sick bird."

"I know a better way to save your trees," said Molly to the man. "Get two hundred

bats and let them loose and they will eat the insects and the birds won't get sick and the fruit will be okay. I saw it on a film. Bats need to eat insects to live."

The man looked surprised. Then he began to laugh.

"Two hundred bats, is it? You girls know a lot," he said.

"We are Pee Wee Scouts," said Molly proudly.

"Well, thank you for the advice," he said.

"You are welcome," said the girls as they walked toward home.

"He might not get the bats," said Mary Beth.

"Well, he stopped spraying, anyway," said Molly.

"I'm going swimming," said Rachel. "See you tomorrow."

The girls waved.

Molly could see it would be a long, hard job to save the earth.

But then no one ever said it was easy, being a Pee Wee Scout.

It was a lot of work.

But it was a lot of fun.

Pee Wee Scout Song

(to the tune of
"Old MacDonald Had a Farm")

Scouts are helpers, Scouts have fun,
Pee Wee, Pee Wee Scouts!
We sing and play when work is done,
Pee Wee, Pee Wee Scouts!

With a good deed here,
And an errand there,
Here a hand, there a hand,
Everywhere a good hand.

Scouts are helpers, Scouts have fun,
Pee Wee, Pee Wee Scouts!

Pee Wee Scout Pledge

We love our country
And our home,
Our school and neighbors too.

As Pee Wee Scouts
We pledge our best
In everything we do.